NIGHT BEFORE
CHRISTMAS

Sue Carabine
Illustrations by
Shauna Mooney Kawasaki

GIBBS·SMITH
P
PUBLISHER

Salt Lake City

First Edition
10 09 08 07   7 6 5

Published by
Gibbs Smith, Publisher
P.O. Box 667
Layton, Utah 84041

Orders: (1-800) 748-5439
www.gibbs-smith.com

Designed and produced by
   Mary Ellen Thompson—TTA Design
Printed in China

ISBN13: 978-1-58685-086-9
ISBN10: 1-58685-086-5
ISBN 1-58685-121-7/Gift

'Twas the week before Christmas.
Santa put on his vest,
His thoughts on a cowgirl way
out in the West.

She had written a letter—
the longest he'd got—
And St. Nick didn't know
if he could help her or not.

"Dear Santa," it started,
"I'm down in the dumps,
And my rear end is covered
in bruises and bumps,

"I was ridin' the herd,
puttin' cowboys to shame,
When my pony's hoof slipped
and the colt came up lame.

"I flew off that horse,
landed down in the dirt,
And the cowpokes was laughin'
until their sides hurt.

"But I'll bet you're a-wonderin'
what this letter's for—
It's a gift that I'm needin',
just one and no more.

"Could I get a man, please,
someone I deserve?
I'll cook and I'll clean
and then he'll ride herd!

"I wouldn't be writin'
this letter, 'cept Slim
(he's my buddy) said, 'Rosie,
you must write to him!

"'Cause when we were kids
St. Nick always came through.'
So I took Slim's advice
and I'm writin' to you.

"'Y' know, Christmas was always
my favorite time,
Would ya get me a man, Nick,
one right in his prime?"

Santa smiled to himself
as he stroked his white beard.
Could he help with this problem?
'Twas a tough one, he feared.

"A true cowboy husband
is what this girl needs,"
His blue eyes, they twinkled,
and he continued to read:

"There's all kinds of cowboys,
some shy and some wild,
I need one in the middle,
part frisky, part mild.

"A cowpoke once asked me
if I'd be his wife,
But ropin' a steer was
the thrill of *his* life.

"He promised his love
would be true till he dies,
Then he marched through my
parlor, boots full of cow pies!"

"Slim says, 'That's natural—
manure's our life's blood.
Don't give up on him, girl,
'cause his boots tread some mud!'

"Then later another dude
asked for my hand.
A chuck wagon cook,
he had already planned

"To cook all the food—
I could picture this scene:
Those meals would be mostly
black coffee and beans!

"Again Slim advised me,
'Gee, what a great life.
Hang on to him, Rosie,
he'll make a great wife!'

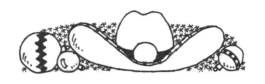

"That Slim's a smart aleck,
just won't mind his ways.
I'll rope, throw an' tie him,
Nick, one of these days!"

After reading 'bout Slim,
St. Nick reminisced
On many fine ranch houses
down on his list.

He'd land close to chimneys
and slide down like silk,
And on hearths he'd find beans
'stead of cookies and milk!

FOR SANTA

But that was okay,
Santa loved western folk,
So he grinned and got back
to the letter she wrote.

Now Rosie got all kinds
of offers, it seems,
But not one of them close
to the man of her dreams.

"The most corny proposal
I got, I should say,
Occurred when I grabbed
forty winks in the hay.

"I heard all of a sudden
this heart-stoppin' din—
A cowboy was tryin'
to sing his way in!

"Now I love western music,
Nick, don't get me wrong,
But this feller he yodeled
and moaned all day long!

"Slim says, 'Rosie, be grateful,
he'll sing you to sleep,
You'll be so darned weary,
you won't count no sheep.'

"Hope yer not tired
of my whinin', St. Nick,
But a couple of others
you should know about quick.

"This dude comes along,
he was all fancied up—
With a pink silk bandana,
herb tea in his cup!

"His Stetson was purple,
the hatband bright green,
And the fanciest boots
he wore outside his jeans!

"The fringe on his jacket
went down to his calf.
I 'bout busted my gut
tryin' hard not to laugh!

"He asked me to dance,
showin' off his loud clothes,
And I swear, when it ended
he'd broke two of my toes!

"Tho' I tried to avoid him,
he kept hangin' on,
Convinced that I loved him,
that yuppie named John.

"I hobbled on home
with an ache in each limb—
I'm 'fraid I can't tell ya
what Slim said 'bout him!

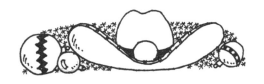

"Now one thing 'bout Slim,
he sure dresses real nice,
'Specially on Sundays
when he smells of Old Spice!

"Well, last but not least
was this gunslinger Ace,
He meant no real harm
but he shot up my place!

"Storms in when he sees me—
I'm bakin' some pies—
Then shoots with both barrels
to kill off some flies!

"I was so gosh durn lucky
to escape with my life.
Yeah, my days would be numbered
if I were his wife!

"Why can't men be like horses,
one of those I could win?
I'd be sweet, kind and gentle
as I'm breakin' him in.

"Well, Santa, I've come
to the end of my tale,
Perhaps as the wife
of a cowboy I'd fail,

"But I'll leave it to you,
dear St. Nick, if you'll try
To find someone out there
who may be the right guy!"

Nick knew right away
who would risk life and limb
To get hitched to this cowgirl—
of course, it was Slim!

He'd been there for Rosie
through good times and bad,
With helpful advice, though
she'd sometimes got mad.

So Nick corralled Slim,
put a word in his ear,
Made him promise to call
in his full cowboy gear.

Santa knew she would give
Slim a wary reception,
But if he wore Old Spice,
she'd make an exception.

So, the night before Christmas
in this cowgirl's town,
She walked down the aisle
in her white wedding gown,

On the arm of her cowboy
whose smile was just beamin',
Outside the snow fallin'
on this bright crispy evenin'.

Nick caught the "I do's"
as he flew by the church,
Quite happy that Rosie
had finished her search.

He called o'er the ranch house
while soaring in flight,
"Merry Christmas, dear cowgirl,
have sweet dreams tonight!"